Text copyright © 2024 by Amy K. Rosenthal GST Exempt Family Trust
Cover art and interior illustrations copyright © 2024 by Brigette Barrager

Written by Christy Webster
Illustrations by Chiara Fiorentino

All rights reserved. Published in the United States by Random House Children's Books,
a division of Penguin Random House LLC, New York.

Random House and the colophon are registered trademarks of Penguin Random House LLC.

Visit us on the Web!
rhcbooks.com

Educators and librarians, for a variety of teaching tools, visit us at RHTeachersLibrarians.com

Library of Congress Cataloging-in-Publication Data is available upon request.
ISBN 978-0-593-65178-0 (trade) — ISBN 978-0-593-65179-7 (lib. bdg.) — ISBN 978-0-593-65180-3 (ebook)

MANUFACTURED IN CHINA
10 9 8 7 6 5 4 3 2 1

Uni the UNICORN

Easter Bunny Helper

an Amy Krouse Rosenthal book
written by Christy Webster
pictures based on art by Brigette Barrager

Random House 🏠 New York

It was the first warm day of the year. Uni the unicorn was visiting a friend, enjoying the breezy weather, when . . .

On the way back to the land of unicorns,
Uni heard a rustling sound.

The egg hunt was the little girl's favorite.
Uni really wanted to help.

Uni looked around, wondering where to begin.

Now where did the little girl say she finds the eggs?

Uni hurried to collect an egg. But . . .

Uni took a peek. . . .

The eggs were plain and white.
They were nothing like the bright
spring colors Uni had seen all day.
Then Uni had an idea.